SOUL CHASER

Raven's Journey

Nicholette Campbell

ISBN: 0692284249
ISBN 13: 9780692284247
Library of Congress Control Number: 2014911727
Nicholette/Campbell
Sweetwater, Tennessee

PROLOGUE

A person's life is quite clear; you're born, you live your life, and you die. It's quite simple and not open for negotiation, but what if you could choose? Most would choose to be born again or to live their life again, but who would choose to die again? Not many and none I had ever encountered. I was born with a purpose in life that few would desire, but I have been fortunate enough to live my life and live again as others. My life started out as all do, with a birth, but my life and death were not of my choosing. Soon I would discover exactly why I'd been born, or *chosen*. I'm sixteen-year-old Raven Bishop, and my life begins and ends with a death. *Mine.*

"It is in your moments of decision that your destiny is shaped."
—Anthony Robbins

1

THE BEGINNING

"Summer, I've been calling for you. What would you like for breakfast?" My mother's voice drifted down the hall, invading my thoughts.

"Waffles," I answered and attempted to push the flashing memories out of my thoughts.

My mother, for the moment, was an exquisitely beautiful woman in her late thirties with dark alabaster eyes and long chestnut-colored hair. She had a bright, beaming smile, high cheekbones, and deep wrinkles from a hard-lived life. She appeared to be of American Indian descent, and so far she was one of my favorites. I'd had several mother figures in my chaotic flashing-forward and flashing-back life, but Paige, my mother for the last few days, was a pure delight to be around.

"Waffles," she said as she entered my room.

"Yes, Paige." Damn, I'd meant to say "Mother." It was difficult to remember the rules, but fortunately she hadn't caught my mistake. So many rules to keep up with and all of them to protect the families I'd encounter on my journey. A journey I still didn't quite understand, but a journey I had to continue to endure while I was still being, or living, or whatever this was. Rules I could not break—*laws*, my spiritual guide had called them once—that I must follow without fail, or an end was inevitable, and I would be no more. Sometimes an end to this madness would be welcomed, but not when I had a mother like this one.

I don't recall my early transformations as a soul chaser. I'd been chosen by divine force to intercept the deaths of innocent children and prevent them from experiencing the pain and agony of death. Fortunately the moment I entered a new body and the spirit departed, most memories from past experiences disappeared. I wouldn't remember who I had been or know who I would become when I entered the new figure, but I could without a doubt remember the previous death. I could recall how I had died and the enormous pain I'd felt as I was murdered, as illness consumed me, or as my life was cut short by tragedy, and it crippled me. It was my curse, or my blessing, but the moment it happened, I'd become a new person awaiting a new demise. Why I was chosen, or cursed, is beyond me; perhaps I was simply being punished for a crime against nature in some bizarre way. The heartache of this life, however, was the end, the last few precious seconds of one's life, waiting for death to come, for the pain to end, for my soul to leave the body and flash again to do this time and time again. I can't recall how many lives I've lived and I don't know how many more deaths I'll have to endure until this madness ends, but I'm certain I've experienced more than a dozen. Some are calm, peaceful even, but most are violent and horrendous and have begun to scare me and more so my spirit. I am starting to remember things now, awful things—not just the deaths—and most things are more terrifying than the end itself. I've found, however, a small bit of comfort in the compassion I felt from the people who loved me while I was theirs. When the memories first started to occur, I was terrified. I didn't want to remember any of it, especially the deaths, but over time I learned I could relive the pleasant moments of my memories, and I'd find myself and a small piece of salvation. I started to cherish the love I'd felt from the guardians of these children and discovered I could see past the anguish of the nightmare to a place of hope. Regrettably, in time, however, breaking the laws has made it difficult to decipher what thoughts are present and what thoughts are recurring memories of the souls I've possessed.

These are complications I long for Lucas to attend to, but unfortunately, his soul was the first one I took control of—so I believed. He had been a beautiful and courageous fourteen-year-old at the time of the transition. Lucas was a soul chaser, and when the conclusion of his own journey approached, he was able to face the end with composure, grace, and a sense of completion as he/I drowned in the community pool. Because of the act of obedience he maintained during his journey, he had been rewarded—a distinctive reward—for following the appropriate laws set before us. After the conversion was complete, it was he who became my guide, a spiritual beacon who selected the next soul to perish, and an enforcer, whose unique purpose was to certify that the laws were obeyed. His death was my birth into the life of soul chasing, and as horrific as it was for me, it's still the one significant moment I hold on to, for that was the one brief moment our souls crossed paths and I came to know my destiny. It was a destiny that would surely end when I could flash no more and met my death. For the momentary seconds our souls were one, Lucas conveyed to me my journey and imparted my laws: never cherish the family you're with, never feel compassion for the soul you're taking, never recall memories of the pleasant experiences, and beyond all others, never reveal the knowledge of your impeding death. Lucas would oversee my journey and only intervene if the laws were not being followed accordingly. Any violation of these laws would warrant a punishment and a fate greater than death.

I often wonder how many souls Lucas possessed before he met his demise and how many more I'll encounter before I meet the same fate. Would someone replace me, as I did Lucas? Did he ever break the laws or conduct himself in a way that a replacement was necessary, or had he paid the ultimate price? Would I get the opportunity to complete my journey, or could I be the end of this mayhem because I've broken too many laws? I may never discover the answers to these concerns, and I've certainly never thought about facing my own death, but clearly I have been in violation of those laws. I'd violated nearly every law with no remorse, and inevitably I would soon be forced to face a punishment.

2

SUMMER

Paige Poole was the kindest and most compassionate woman I'd ever met and a magnificent mother to Summer. She was completely devoted to her daughter's every want and need and had given more of herself to her daughter than any other mother I'd encountered on my journey. She'd showered Summer with love and overbearing protection, but gave her the freedom to be a child. She'd guarded and shielded her from all forms of harm, so it was truly devastating to accept that soon she would lose her only child, a child she loved wholeheartedly. She would do anything to save her or gladly trade places with her if she knew what was to come.

I'd never before felt sorrow for the soul I was taking, but more often than not I felt enormous pain for the ones losing their beloved. The heartache they felt in knowing a loved one was gone forever and the blessing of their presence lost. The gaping hole left in their hearts, the tears shed, the loneliness left by the departed, and the desperation to keep that person's memory alive. The challenges they'd face as their sense of security and confidence in the predictability of life faded. Although the overwhelming need for closure consumed them, the thought of losing a child was unimaginable and unbearable still, even to me.

It was unmistakably the same each time: a parent was losing a child, a grandparent was losing a grandchild, or some other relative was losing a young member of the family. Nevertheless, without fail, it would always be a child or adolescent I died for, never an adult. Possibly there was an age limit to this madness. Maybe their minds were just too closed to the possibilities, or perhaps children were innocent enough that they should never endure the pain of death. Whatever the reasoning, it was my burden to face death and the uncertainty of pain or peace that unfolded in front of me.

Summer's story was completely different from the others. She was the youngest child I had ever died for thus far; she was merely eight years old when I took control of her body. She was such a beautiful little girl—big, lively hazel eyes and long, curly bronze hair, and an angelic face with olive-toned skin and the same high cheekbones her mother had. She seemed small for her age, but physically she appeared healthy. She never uttered a sound as her soul left her body, nor did her spirit linger as so many often did when I transformed into them. As Summer calmly and gracefully drifted to the unknown, I felt calm for once instead of the usual horrid panic. This was the first and only peaceful moment of transition I'd encounter on Summer's journey. Death would be terribly violent and scarring moment for me, it turned out.

My life as Summer started out as others did. I quickly immersed myself into her life, learning as much as possible about her family, friends, and anything else of importance for my time there. Paige, Summer's mother, loved telling stories about her daughter, so she was a great help to me without her knowing it. I heard countless stories about Summer, her childhood, and her family's home: a small white farmhouse with rustic shutters and a broken-down picket fence in the front yard and an old tire swing hanging from a great white oak in the back. That old tree was the very place Paige had found Summer crying when Benjamin, Summer's father, had left them when she was only four and again only a year later when Paige told her only child that her favorite maternal grandmother had passed. Summer had dealt with more loss than any other child at such a young age should have had to tolerate, and her father's sudden abandonment had taken its toll. She'd never fully recovered. I'd felt the pain of rejection the moment I entered her body; I knew the feeling well, for I too had been abandoned as a child.

I learned a great deal those first few days about Summer's family and all the tragedies they'd overcome, but the one thing I found troubling was how a man could leave his wife and beautiful little girl. Something felt odd about it; what made him choose this? Did he choose this? Paige never talked about Benjamin, so I had no way of knowing or even finding out, but for the strangest reason, I felt an urgency to know why. Maybe then, I'd be able to figure out why I was here taking Summer's place in death. It was too late for her to make peace with it, but hopefully Paige would find comfort in knowing, or perhaps she'd always known and simply kept it from Summer to protect her. As my destiny unfolded, I soon came face to face with the truth and discovered exactly why he'd been forced out of their lives forever.

3

A FATHER'S BETRAYAL

A mother's love knows no bounds, and Paige would prove to be no exception. We had spent the better part of our Saturday at the park, watching children play with their families and sharing a picnic lunch on a red and white flannel blanket. We enjoyed the peanut butter and jelly sandwiches, which were Summer's favorite, according to Paige. Once our lunch was consumed, Paige wanted to walk around the borders of the park, picking daises and lilies and talking. She wanted to really talk about a number of things, strange things; we talked about life and death, and how truly devastated she'd be if something ever happened to her Summer. We even discussed Benjamin, which quite frankly disturbed me and increased the urgency to uncover the truth about him. Secretly I wondered why she had chosen this moment to bring him up, considering we'd just been discussing loss and despair. Once again I found myself questioning why he'd chosen to leave them in the first place. She had never been so open with me, and I was beginning to wonder if she'd somehow discovered the truth about me. I quickly dismissed that thought when she turned and kissed me on the forehead with tears in her eyes and said, "I love you, Summer."

With that, I broke yet another rule and repeated the sentiment. "I love you too, Momma."

"Eat your waffles, Summer," Paige kept saying as we sat facing each other at our small cobblestone-finished kitchen table. Her voice finally broke through my rambling thoughts and brought me back to the reality I was in. Sitting there with this loving woman, both of us still in our fleecy pink PJs and fuzzy white slippers, would be a moment I'd long for by the night's end. I'm never surprised when death finds me, but the end of Summer Poole's life gave new significance to the words fatal and tragic and gave true meaning to a mother's sacrifice and undying love for her daughter.

I remember it quite clearly, as I do most deaths, the chain of events that spun horribly out of control; however, the repulsive parts were the ones I'd try to omit from my memories. Unfortunately, this death would be another monumentally scarring moment for me, but the moments before the end would torment even the most evil demon to roam this planet. I'm quite certain a small part of me died that afternoon, right along with Summer.

The morning started off sunny and peaceful. We were enjoying our breakfast of waffles and orange juice, with the smell of freshly cut grass floating on a cool spring breeze from the window. But a sense of dread started to surround me as the morning dragged on, and the once-bright smile on Paige's face faded when a call came in and she noticed the number on her cell phone. She'd cleared the dishes from the table and nervously paced the length of the wooden kitchen floor watching the front door. We'd both been startled by the repeated—more than necessary—banging on the back door and alarmed by a man's yelling voice that followed.

As Paige opened the door, a stream of profanity—"damn you" and "go to hell" and words too vulgar for an eight-year-old to hear—came pouring into the room as a man over six feet tall rushed in. He grabbed Paige by the throat and then zeroed in on me. Me, the frail child in her pink fleece PJs whose life had already ended, stared back into those once emerald-colored, now darkened, bloodshot eyes. The room was electric and silent, hot and frigid, and bright and dark all at the same time as Paige desperately tried to reach out for me in a failed attempt. The man, a massive stranger, dressed in a dingy, stained T-shirt and ragged jeans with bloody bare feet, had now also grabbed Paige's arm by the elbow and thrust it back behind her with his free hand. Paige's shoulders were arched, but her back was almost completely flush against the man's chest, and he was whispering something in her ear through gritted teeth. He continued to stare directly at me. The smell of whiskey and cigar smoke was distinct in the air; the aroma was nauseating, but somehow I found my voice.

"Momma," I pleaded.

The laughter that echoed from the man's chest was utterly chilling, and in a most unnatural way, the sinister smile on his face seemed to touch his eyes, causing the slightest break in his stare. "No, Daddy's home," he said in a baleful, matter-of-fact way.

Before I could halt the words from exiting my mouth, I'd spoken. "Benjamin?"

To my complete dismay, I watched the cobra-tight grip of his fingers loosen a fraction from Paige's throat. The temporary slip fueled his anger and my fear but gave Paige a split second to mouth the word "Run!"

Run was a simple word with so many meanings: run for help, run out of fear or desire to live, or run for protection from this monster, but running from death was something I couldn't do. I'd never run before; death had always found me so easily, and I was always certain when the end was near. So the notion of escaping this death or any other was impossible to imagine. I was not going to survive this, and neither was Summer; she was already gone. But Paige—why was this happening to Paige? What kind of betrayal would fuel this kind of madness and mayhem?

The sound of ice being dropped into a glass snapped my thoughts back to the scene before me. Benjamin had bound Paige's hands and feet together with her favorite "Kiss the Cook" apron and beaten her so badly that she was in the fetal position on the floor of our kitchen. Her head was cocked to one side, and I could see the wetness on her face. Blood or tears, I couldn't be sure, but she was deathly silent. Her eyes were wide open, but she stared at nothing. She was breathing; I was sure of that. I watched the slow rhythmic motion of her chest rising and falling. I found comfort in that and that alone, because the monster was still here and now moving toward me with catlike precision. I closed my eyes and sensed his approach and then felt the pain, the teeth-rattling blow to my cheek, and the ringing in my ears as his hand made contact.

This vile man had slapped his only child and was now demanding I look at him. Fighting back vomit and tears, I did as I was told and looked him square in the eyes.

"You're a brave little bitch, aren't you? Maybe I should teach you some manners," he said and once again found my cheek with his fist. This time he knocked me completely out of my chair and onto the floor next to Paige. I tried desperately to reach out to her, but Benjamin, now standing over the top of us, grabbed me by my hair and lifted me off the floor just above my mother's limp, broken body. I could now clearly see the blood on her face.

"Momma," I pleaded, but she remained lifeless and still. "Please, Benjamin, why are you doing this?"

"Ask your mother," he spat as that evil, sadistic laughter started again. "I'm your father, and you will respect me as such, do you understand?"

"No, never!" I cried out.

The rage consumed him once more. The next thought to register in my conscious mind was that I was flying through the air and slamming into the wall on the other side of the room. When the daze cleared and I was able to open my eyes, the entire atmosphere had changed and the smell of smoke burned my nostrils. The front half of the kitchen was ablaze, and the fire was edging closer.

Paige and I were now bound and lying on the kitchen floor facing away from each other. I could barely see anything because the smoke was so thick. I could hear Benjamin hammering on the entry door of the kitchen; he was nailing the doors shut. I again tried desperately to reach out to Paige; I needed to know she was alive. I was unable to move anything but my head from side to side. My leather restraints had been tied in an unusual way. My hands were tied behind my back and my feet were tied together, but the straps had been tied to each other so my body was in a contorted backward *C*. The ache in my back was grueling, but I had to try. I had to reach her to save her life.

My destiny was clear; my fate was to die for Summer. I'd died at the hands of murderers before; I'd been beaten to death, shot point-blank, and stabbed repeatedly, but I'd always been alone. I'd never had to fear for another individual being harmed. Those monsters had taken me, and my purpose was fulfilled. I'd never felt terror or panic but simple completion as my spirit flashed again.

But now an uncanny sense of horror gripped me, and I needed to act swiftly. The smoke was nearly unbearable as it burning my lungs, and the heat from the far side of the kitchen was blazing hot and getting closer. The flames were shooting higher and consuming everything in their path. It was clearly the end for me, but why Paige? I was desperate to get her out, to keep her safe. With the last lungful of air I could breathe, I began yelling, "Mom! Mom! Paige! Paige, please, can you hear me? You have to get out. Hurry, you have to get out!"

"Summer." The first panicked word I'd heard Paige say was followed by a fit of coughing and gagging and then silence once more.

4

A MOTHER'S SACRIFICE

I'd always heard that smoke inhalation would kill you before the flame reached you, but in the case of Paige and Summer Poole, that statement couldn't be more false.

The smell of hair burning was horrible, but the stench of burning flesh was sickening and mentally scarring. The only hope I had to save Paige from the raging inferno was to burn the straps I was bound in. The far side of the kitchen was fully engulfed in red and blue flames, and the room was blackened by smoke, but I had to save her. She would have given her life for her daughter if she was capable, but Summer's fate was sealed. My destiny was being fulfilled, but she didn't have to die, not at the hands of the man she'd clearly tried to protect me from.

When Benjamin had the windows and all but the final door nailed shut, he entered the room to admire his workmanship; he wanted to make sure we wouldn't escape. He stood in the entryway of the only exit available to us and glared at Paige. What could she have possibly done to this evil man to meet this fate? Could this be the reason he'd left or been forced away? This violent man, hell bent on destroying a mother and child, felt no guilt or remorse, only pure amusement at his destructive actions.

I'd not heard a sound or seen any movement from Paige since that last panicked word, and I was certain death was coming. The fire was closing in on her, and she'd been struggling for breath when she'd last called out to me. If I didn't take action now, she would burn alive—if she was still alive. I couldn't see anything, but I could hear what sounded to me like a violent struggle coming from where I thought she was. She was alive and fighting Benjamin to save herself.

The next few things that occurred happened in fast-forward. I don't know how Paige had managed it, but there she was, kneeling next to me and trying to untie my strap. Most of her long chestnut hair was melted, some of it completely gone and other parts still smoking. Her eyebrows and eyelashes were completely gone, and her hands were so badly scorched from burning off her straps that a few of her fingers were fused together. Her once fuzzy PJs were now unrecognizable; they were completely melted onto her skin, and the flesh from her forehead appeared to be falling from her skull. Miraculously she'd found the strength to overpower Benjamin for a brief moment in an attempt to save her daughter.

"Hurry, Summer. We have to hurry," Paige said in a chillingly calm voice as I felt her being jerked away. Both she and I were still reaching out for one another when Benjamin tossed her frail body across the room like a football. The loud thud and flash of flames confirmed my worst fears. Paige was dead. This poor woman, whose only crime was protecting her daughter, had fallen prey to this murderous man, my father.

As the forbidden tears started falling from my eyes, there was nothing I could do to stop them. Even if I'd been able to control my emotions, I didn't want to. This was entirely too much for anyone to witness. No one should watch his or her mother die; even if she wasn't my actual mother, I'd grown fond of Paige, and I adored her. For the first time in my life, I felt love from a mother. As I turned my face to wipe the tears away, I caught sight of Benjamin walking toward me through the smoke with that sadistic look on his face.

I was not going to give him the satisfaction of begging for my life; my fate was sealed. I was there to die for Summer, and that's exactly what I was doing now, dying. Pain was clawing and ripping at my throat and not allowing the breath to get in. The smoke was too heavy, but begging would serve no purpose. My destiny was being fulfilled as it should have been. I certainly didn't enjoy dying continuously, and I'd never found comfort in the pain of death, but it was me living these horrific events and not the innocent children death intended to claim. However, Benjamin's demanding looks were asking for just that: for me to beg and plead for mercy and for my life to be spared. He lifted me to my feet and cradled me in his arms before whispering the words that confirmed why he'd been forced away.

"They should have never let me out," he coldly stated, more so to himself than me. "You want to live, Summer?"

I simply closed my eyes, knowing he was toying with me. I was going to die, and I wouldn't give him the pleasure of asking for anything.

"Summer, do you want to live?"

His words were drawing the vomit from my stomach again, but I somehow managed the words to ensure I got exactly what I wanted the most. "I want my mother, Benjamin!"

The last thing I recall is being dumped from his lap and the sound of him storming out of the kitchen before nailing the final door shut from the outside. In this inferno of our kitchen, I thought, *Let the laws be damned,* and I whispered to Paige, "I love you." I died that morning, burned alive. Death by fire was my fate as Summer's body turned back into ash. Flash!

5

LUCAS

As Raven's guide, I watched her struggle with her transition for some time, and soon I would be forced to intervene. Her spirit would no longer tolerate the emotional turmoil she was inflicting on herself. She would be a trapped soul indefinitely if she couldn't find a sense of contentment or gain a complete understanding of her journey. My own guide had been forced to intervene at the beginning of my journey. I'd been selfish too, but he'd warned me of my consequences: any violation of the laws would result in a life of confinement as a soul chaser. I'd been given a second chance, and I vowed not to squander the opportunity. Becoming a soul chaser is quite a difficult conversion but a genuine blessing once you acknowledge the requirements and embrace your destiny. Raven's constant struggle, however, was more than I could have envisioned or expected. Compassion was an obstacle I'd never considered when I chose her. She could not see past the anguish of death to the place of necessity.

I'd been a soul chaser for years; dying for children was all I had ever known. Of course I'd felt empathy for them, but this was my destiny, and I embraced the challenge with selflessness. A child's life and death are predetermined, and no amount of compassion would alter that. I'd been chosen to endure the deaths of the most innocent and allow their spirits to move on to the afterlife. Once I understood and accepted the reasoning behind why I had been chosen, I felt honor each time a soul departed. They'd never have to experience the horrific pain of dying or the risk of becoming lost as their spirits simply slipped away; their souls would quietly drift to the heavens as I took possession of their bodies and faced their untimely deaths.

Most children born into this world live ordinary lives; they face challenging events throughout the course of their lives, but they lived as they should, growing into adulthood, discovering the purpose of their lives, and perishing as intended. There would be no reason for their souls to linger on earth. They'd feel complete as their spirits moved on. Regrettably in this world there are also those children who are damned from the beginning, simply being born to the wrong person or circumstances and never living long enough to fulfill their purpose. A murder, an illness, or another tragedy would cut their life short, and their soul would forever be trapped, searching for closure—never moving forward and never moving back, just wandering the earth as a lost spirit.

My soul had been imprisoned this way; I'd never had the opportunity to uncover the purpose of my life. I'd tragically drowned in the community pool on my fourteenth birthday. I was trapped in a state of purgatory, wandering the earth until Marcus, my spiritual guide, chose me. He'd conveyed my journey and imparted my laws as my spirit was released to retrieve the souls of displaced spirits. If the soul departed a child's body before the experience of death found him or her, the soul would bypass purgatory. The child would be reunited with the heavens, and his or her life would be complete. An untimely death was the binding factor between freedom and confinement.

I'd died far too early to fulfill the purpose of my life, but preventing a child from suffering the struggles of exile and isolation would comfort me until my soul moved on. I would chase the souls of children who could potentially be lost to purgatory until my journey ended and my life was completed. When my spirit had aged to my true, intended time of death, I would choose my replacement, and my spirit would be freed. I would move on to guide the next soul chaser, as Marcus had told me, until his or her destiny was fulfilled. Then I too would pass on to the afterlife. My replacement would choose a successor when his or her journey was complete, and the process would be repeated until the necessity was no longer required.

The end of my journey was approaching rather quickly, and I had yet to choose my replacement. The requirements were clear. Candidates had to be children who had died or were going to die an untimely death. Children who were free to move on would not be chosen. There would be no just cause for them to wander once their spirit was settled in the afterlife; they'd not be among the lost spirits of the world. The successor had to maintain discretion and follow all abiding rules. If the guardian of a child foresaw the death and attempted to intervene, the child would be lost and subjected to purgatory for eternity. A soul chaser could not guide an adult to the afterlife under any circumstance. Candidates had to complete their journey and restrain all emotion for the children; our destiny was one of retrieval, not damnation. All deaths are predetermined, and our purpose was to simply allow the spirit to move onward. If you chose a candidate who had already faced his or her death before selection, that candidate should have not viewed their lifeless body at the time of death or as the spirit disengaged the remains. If a child saw his or her body after death, the child would be overcome with the despairing thoughts of their death. The spirit would forever be in turmoil; the question of *why* their death occurred would consume them, and that consumption would be their eternal state of purgatory. The spirit would always be lost. Due to the unsettled state of the spirit, the soul could never be chosen. However, a child who never saw their lifeless body after death would simply be in a state of confusion----as I had been----- the child would not comprehend that his or her death had actually occurred.

If you choose a successor who had not yet faced his or her death, you had to intervene the instant the spirit detached from the body to prevent viewing, per the above requirement. These were the absolute requirements for all candidates.

I'd considered all the requirements and felt confident in my capability to choose an adequate replacement. Marcus would oversee my decision but refrain from interfering. He would monitor my conversion from soul chaser to spiritual guide; then his soul would be free to move on. I would be left alone with my choice and all repercussions of that decision. If I failed to choose a satisfactory replacement who met and followed the requirements, I could once again be facing a life of confinement. My spirit would never advance beyond what I was now, a displaced spirit, and the child chosen would cease to exist entirely. There could be no redemption for continuous failure.

6

ELIJAH

Lucas's warning was in my thoughts when I heard a Tick-tock, tick-tock sound; a clock was ticking nearby to the beat of my heart. I hadn't yet opened my eyes; the feeling of being burned alive crowded my mind. The stench of burning flesh was etched into my memory forever. My life as Summer Poole was over, but could I possibly bear another lost life so soon? I'd faced death without fear numerous times, but the last and most gruesome had scarred me, I was certain, indefinitely. I'd grown accustomed to being able to dismiss, or at least partly dismiss, the details of a person's life—except for wondering why I was living these tragic events—but nothing of the last few days made any sense to me. I remembered everything, and unfortunately it was time to open my eyes to assume the soul of yet another young person and face his or her catastrophic death with no regard for my present state or sanity.

Whenever I opened my eyes for the first time as a new person, I'd always been alone, possibly by coincidence, but I was comfortable with that, simply because it actually gave me a moment to examine my surroundings and assess my approximate age and gender. Unfortunately, my experience this time was far different from anything I'd dealt with before. As I opened my eyes, I found I wasn't alone; I was enveloped by a room full of people all staring at me as if I had two heads, and at that moment, I possibly could have.

I was afraid to speak or breathe, let alone allow my eyes to focus on the crowd that moved closer as I blinked rapidly, watching its every move. The man who was sitting on the edge of the bed closest to me, holding something pale, seemed the most intent. His dark, strained eyes against his pale, battered skin were startling; however, I noticed right away that he was holding a frail, little hand with what appeared to be an IV in it. Once the circuits of my brain kicked in, I realized it was me he was holding.

"Elijah, don't talk," the man commanded as I heard an almost inaudible noise coming from my throat.

I was Elijah, a boy, a tiny boy in a hospital bed. Could I be dying already? This would certainly be a change, dying within moments of transforming into a new body. Perhaps this would be easier, no pretending or acclimating, just fulfilling my purpose here: death.

The tick-tock sound I mistook as a clock earlier caught my attention first; it wasn't a clock at all but a machine on the right side of me that monitored each one of my heartbeats. The rhythmic sound seemed to keep the room from bursting at the seams with each beep, beep, beep and how dark the room was with only a soft light coming from a lamp across the room. I could just barely make out balloons and a stuffed toy of some sort sitting on the table behind two young women, but I was sure there were flowers. I could smell those—lilies and daises, some of my favorite scents over the years, each of them being, at some point in the past, one of the last fragrances to enter my consciousness before death found me.

"Elijah, how are you feeling today?"

The voice I heard from the chipper old man walking into the room caught my attention immediately, but the reaction from the man still holding my hand warned me I shouldn't try to respond.

"He shouldn't be speaking, Dr. Hartley; he isn't well," the man cautioned.

"Thomas, Elijah is doing great today, and you mustn't keep him confined like this," the doctor said cheerfully. "He needs some sunshine."

Dr. Hartley proceeded to open the white miniblinds to reveal the morning sun brightly shining outside. I was finally able to distinguish all the people who crowded the small hospital room, and clearly the man still grasping my hand was not pleased with the doctor in the slightest.

"Thomas, Elijah is a tough little boy, and he will beat this. He's done it once before, and it appears he's doing it again; his blood results look clear. Trust me, leukemia will not be a death sentence, and if he feels up to it, he should be moving around and enjoying his life. You don't want to keep him from living as normally as possible so he has a desire to live when he overcomes this."

The doctor's words did little to ease the tension in the room, but now I knew why I was here. Leukemia was going to be a death sentence for Elijah and another transformation for me. Was this ever going to end for me? Would I always suffer for these children? Could I ever find peace in this world, or would a question of timing change everything?

7

DR. HARTLEY

Dr. Hartley was a breath of fresh air, so uplifting and positive. I'd rarely encountered a man so supportive of and compassionate toward children. On my journey, I'd felt sympathy for the children I was dying for because their lives were over and all possibilities were gone forever, but the laws forbade compassion. Lucas had been clear: any violation of law would result in a great punishment, and I was clearly jeopardizing the outcome of my being with every ounce of empathy I felt for these children. However, when the untimely death of a child became the question, I would gladly take my punishment to ensure a mistake had not been made.

Elijah hadn't hesitated to exit as I entered his spirit, and an overwhelming sense of exhaustion and emptiness flooded me when I took control of his body. There was no question he was gone and I was there to fulfill my destiny. But Dr. Hartley's conviction regarding Elijah's health and well-being was causing me to question how he would die if leukemia wasn't his killer. Could Lucas have misjudged the timing of his death? Was that even possible? I'd never doubted the choices Lucas had made before; he was my guide and I trusted him, but something felt off about the timing or nature of Elijah's death. Dr. Hartley's continuous urge to update Thomas on the possibilities of remission was undeniably a reason for concern.

Dr. William Hartley was possibly in his mid to late sixties and of German descent. His silver hair was receding to form the perfect widow's peak, and his eyes were so dark blue that they almost appeared black. His wrinkled skin showed his age, but his personality was that of a much younger man. I could always smell him before I saw him; the scent of Brut would give him away every time. He never dressed in the typical doctors' apparel but rather in a casual suit with an out-of-place name badge, like you'd see on a visitor at an office or school, and he always had a handful of balloons at the ready in funny shapes or various animals for the children on our ward. I'd not seen him angry or temperamental in the slightest, but I'm sure he was stern; people did as they were told around the good doctor. Maybe it was simply out of respect.

Dr. Hartley was the head of oncology, the chief of pediatrics, and a brilliant man according to the day nurses who took care of Elijah, or me, as it were. I once heard Julia, the head day nurse, tell my father that the great doctor had a passion for healing the sickest of children, and he'd sworn to all that was holy that he would do everything in his power to save a child's life. My father hung onto her every word as she spoke, but I couldn't stop myself from staring at her; something about her looks reminded me of someone in my past.

Julia Stone, RN, was a stunning woman with long, board-straight, red hair; eyes so big and green they appeared to be emerald spheres stuck in the holes where her eyes should be; and freckles on just about every part of her body that was visible. She wore the typical nursing uniform, always pressed and tidy, but she too had that out-of-place name badge. She was a younger woman, possibly mid-twenties, and too youthful looking to have dealt with much tragedy, especially a child's death. By working on this ward, however, she had surely seen a great deal. Her looks and accent suggested she was Irish. This lovely woman was so compassionate to Elijah and Thomas and was constantly making sure we had everything we needed while she was on watch for the day. Dr. Hartley and Julia worked well together; his wisdom and her grace were an uncanny combination of trust, loyalty, and commitment; they truly completed each other.

My journey subjected me to children in their darkest days; their fate was predetermined, and I accepted that. I never had to question whether a child would perish when I took possession of their soul; it was my destiny. Nonetheless, the nature and timing of their death was unclear until death found me. Fortunately I'd never been required to spend a measurable amount of time as any particular child; I died within a few hours or days upon my entry; therefore, I didn't have time to envision the particulars of their lives or their families' lives. I fulfilled my destiny and flashed again to the next departing child, but with Elijah things were uncertain. Upon learning of all the devastation Thomas had endured over the last few years through his constant prayers, I instantly felt admiration for him and sadness for Elijah. Why had Lucas waited so long to intervene? Could he have spared this heartache for Thomas sooner?

Thomas had dealt with death before; Elijah's mother had died giving birth to him, which provided some insight as to why Thomas was so protective and cautious. He'd brought Elijah home from the hospital, sold his landscaping business, and devoted his life to raising his only child. When his first bout with cancer occurred, Elijah was barely two. They practically lost everything, but through it all Thomas fought to keep his son alive. Prior to Elijah going into remission the first time, Thomas's faith had weakened, but his desire to protect his son had grown stronger. He'd done research, donated blood, and volunteered for bone marrow screening, to no avail, but he'd continued to hope and pray for a miracle. He'd met Julia Stone then, and the two became devoted friends; she had just transferred to the hospital where Dr. Hartley was monitoring Elijah weekly. After six long months of countless tests, chemotherapy treatments, and experimental drugs, the young boy went into remission. However, on his one-year checkup, the news was devastating once more: he'd had a relapse. They all were shattered with disbelief. The leukemia had returned, and both Thomas and Julia vowed to fight alongside Elijah to get him back into remission. Following another yearlong battle with countless radiation treatments, blood tests, and painful bone marrow aspirations, could the possibility of remission be in their grasp again?

As minutes turned into hours and hours into days, Elijah's body grew stronger, and all symptoms disappeared, I felt the surge of energy and liveliness of his spirit. Dr. Hartley sensed it as well and promptly ordered the final series of blood tests and bone aspirations to be performed. If Elijah's body had gone back into remission as the doctor suspected, he would be released from the hospital the following morning. He would continue to be monitored weekly for a healthy Complete Blood Count but the prognosis was bright. Only the results would reveal the truth, but somehow I knew. I'd died as a cancer-ridden child before, and Elijah was not one of those children; his little body was healthy and flourishing, and I could feel it.

The hours ticked by as Thomas paced the halls of the hospital and prayed, waiting for the test results to come in. He was optimistic but realistic too. He'd been through this very situation a year ago and knew the heartache of false hope; he would not endure that again. Dr. Hartley was confident the results would show remission, but Thomas needed to be certain. The afternoon sun was setting outside my window when the female laboratory technician walked in and handed Dr. Hartley the news we'd all been awaiting. He could barely contain his exhilaration as he read the words aloud. "Complete remission," he proclaimed as my father burst into tears and grabbed me in a triumphant embrace.

"We're going home, son," he whispered in my ear as he hugged me tighter. The evidence was clear; leukemia was not going to kill Elijah, but what would and when? How much longer would I have to hold it together for the sake of this child?

8

WELCOME HOME

The sky was overcast the morning Elijah got to go home. Despite the dark, dismal morning, everyone's spirits were high. Elijah had beaten cancer twice in his five short years of life, and that was indeed a reason to be joyous. Thomas could hardly contain his excitement as he and Julia packed Elijah's things, preparing to go home. This would be Elijah's first trip home in nearly a year, and Thomas insisted they do something spectacular for the occasion. Dr. Hartley had released Elijah to resume his normal activities and suggested a welcome home party to acclimate him back into everyday life. Thomas was thrilled with the idea and made plans; Julia would take Elijah home with her to rest while Thomas gathered the necessary decorations and gifts. Once Thomas had finished his errands and had the house ready for the party, Julia would bring Elijah home. The party would be a welcome home bash to celebrate Elijah's life and all he'd overcome.

I listened while the plans were being finalized; the type of ice cream was my choice, but Thomas decided the details of the festivities would be a surprise. The feelings of anguish and despair he'd felt a mere day ago were replaced with anticipation and delight. Those strained eyes I first noticed when I'd taken Elijah's place no longer appeared strained in the slightest but were bright and animated. I'd never truly noticed before how attractive Thomas was or the budding relationship that clearly was developing between Julia and him. Thomas had been through hell the last few years, and Julia had journeyed the most recent battle with him; hopefully they'd find comfort in each other when I fulfilled my purpose.

Tears were shed by some and applause rang out from others as Elijah was wheeled from the hospital for the final time. The yearlong battle was over for this little boy, and he was finally going home. Julia had her car parked in front of the patients' exit as Thomas rolled me out the door; the overcast sky had broken for a brief moment to reveal the bright morning sun shining down on us. As we approached the car, I caught my reflection in the window of Julia's car. Elijah was a precious little boy with big, bright-blue eyes and a sweet baby face. Most of his hair was missing due to the chemo treatments, and his skin was still pale, but his chubby cheeks and round dimples reminded me of a cherub you'd see on a holiday card.

I was still gazing at my reflection when Thomas walked up to me and placed his hand on my arm. "My beautiful boy," he said as he leaned down and kissed me on my forehead. Then he whispered, "Let's go home," and lifted me from my chair. He hugged me tightly before climbing into the backseat of Julia's car. He secured my highback booster seat in the middle position of her car so Elijah would be able to see the world he'd missed for nearly a year. Once Thomas was certain I was safely restrained, he kissed the tip of my nose and spoke the last words I'd ever hear him say: "I love you, Elijah. I'll see you soon."

9

BROKEN GLASS

The ride to Julia's house was peaceful. The clouds had finally begun to break, allowing the midmorning sun to peek through from time to time, but the air was still quite brisk—cold even—for mid-spring. Fortunately Julia had been thoughtful enough to bring a flannel blanket to cover my legs. I was excited about discovering the world Elijah had known before his hospitalization; all I'd really known of this sweet little boy was how he'd spent the majority of his life hooked up to one piece of machinery or another to keep his tiny body alive and the overwhelming sense of exhaustion I'd felt as I took control of his body. I wanted to see, touch, and feel everything he'd encountered during his five short years. I wanted to explore his life, but it turned out destiny had other plans for his little body and my existence.

"We're almost home, Elijah. Are you awake? Wake up, sweetie, we'll be home in a few minutes," I heard Julia say. Upon opening my eyes, the first thing I saw were Julia's affectionate green eyes looking back at me. She winked and blew a kiss toward me. I smiled at her and then looked past her at the pickup truck, loaded with steel rods sticking out of the bed of the truck, stopping suddenly in front of us.

"The road!" I screamed, but it was too late. Crash!

The force of impact was devastating; our mini-cruiser had slammed into the truck at forty miles an hour. Who could survive something like this? I yelled out for Julia but got no response. Again I called out to her, and she groaned. "Julia, are you OK? You need to get out."

"Elijah, *do not move*," she commanded.

"I want out, get me out," I pleaded.

"Elijah, listen to me. I am out, sweetie. You're trapped, do you understand?"

"*Paige*, I want out! Get me out."

"Elijah, I cannot move you. Help is on the way. Just hold on, sweetie; you're going into shock. Elijah. Elijah! Don't go to sleep! Stay with me; are you with me, sweetie? Elijah, wake up!"

"*Paige*, my chest hurts. Why does my chest hurt? Did I fall down?"

"Elijah, I'm Julia, can you hear me? We've been in an accident, and you've been hurt."

"Help me, *Paige!*"

I heard the words the moment they came out of my mouth, but I couldn't stop them. This wasn't shock; it was a crossover. My spirit was trying to flash again or flash back, but I hadn't yet passed as Elijah. I was trapped—not just in the car but also in this body—until death found me.

Julia's voice caught my attention and brought me back to the scene surrounding me. The pressure on my chest was crushing. I attempted to move, but her panicked pleas terminated any further adjustments. "Don't move, Elijah," Julia begged, with tears streaming down her face.

"I'm cold," I managed to say and quickly realized my breathing was restricted. As Julia moved the blanket that once covered my legs, I saw the extent of the damage that had been done to Elijah's little body.

The pickup truck we'd collided with had been hauling steel rods inappropriately restrained to the vehicle; therefore, the impact of a rear-end collision turned these simple pieces of metal into flying missiles targeting Elijah's chest, and contact had been made. A steel rod, an inch in diameter, had punctured the windshield, passed through the interior of the car, and found its resting place inside the chest of the five-year-old's body. The amount of blood was minimal for a wound of this magnitude, but the pain was excruciating. Surely death would find me soon. Dr. Hartley had been right; cancer wouldn't kill Elijah, but this certainly would.

A life cut short by illness is grueling, but a life cut short by tragedy is just that: tragic and catastrophic. The sudden onset of sadness and loss for the loved one being left behind is nearly as dire as the death itself. No closure or final words spoken to the dearly departed, just emptiness and pain. Thomas would soon face that very lonely place, and again I felt compelled to question why Lucas had waited so long to intervene. Couldn't he have taken Elijah sooner and spared Thomas this new burden?

Sirens in the distance snapped me back to reality. A chaotic swarm of bystanders had gathered around the mangled wreckage. The panicked disbelief and horror I saw on most faces clearly indicated how grievous my injuries truly were.

"Is he alive?" a woman called out as Julia placed her fingers on my wrist. She'd somehow managed to crawl across the broken glass and twisted metal to my left side.

"He's got a pulse, but it's weak. Where's that ambulance," she shouted back. "Elijah, can you hear me? Your dad's on his way, sweetie. Just stay with me."

I couldn't respond. The rod pressing against my lungs had practically blocked the air from entering my body; therefore, breathing deep enough to form a response was impossible. With no oxygen moving in and no oxygen moving out, this tiny body would fail soon. I could feel my consciousness fading when Julia started humming a soft melody to comfort me as I awaited death. I focused my eyes on her and noticed the bloody gash in the middle of her forehead. Julia had been hurt too; I wanted to reach out to her and comfort her the way she was comforting me; I had to try.

The instant I lifted my arm to reach out, my shoulder shifted to the left a fraction of a centimeter; I felt the cold metal rod respond to the motion. Instantaneous pain radiated throughout my body as I gasped for breath. The tiny shift had caused the rod to knick my lung, and I was bleeding out. Julia desperately cried out for help, but it was too late. I died that afternoon, staring into her eyes with an overwhelming sense of exhaustion. Flash.

10

DEATH AND CONSEQUENCES

Raven was a child facing an untimely death when I chose her. I selected a child who had yet to face her own death; I would not jeopardize my salvation with unnecessary risks. Raven was going to drown as I had; the similarities we shared aided my decision. Her body would die in time as mine did, but she would not yet be required to endure the sacrifice of her own death. I would shoulder the burden for her. I would die in her place as I had for so many others, but she would not move on to the afterlife; she would take my place as a soul chaser. She would only be required to face the death of her body and experience the emotional struggles of succumbing to her own death if she violated the rules set before her. She would continue on her journey until her destiny was fulfilled and she chose her own successor.

When I flashed into Raven's body, our souls crossed paths. I conveyed her journey and imparted her laws. Choosing her to become a soul chaser would keep her spirit viable and allow her to experience an abundance of time with a purpose that had forsaken her while she was among the living. The moment her soul departed, I became a guide, and Marcus was finally free to journey on to the heavens. Raven had reluctantly flashed onward to retrieve the first soul of many she'd assist on her journey. Her spirit seemed to be conflicted, and I neglected to recognize her distress. I should have seen her hesitancy. We protected children from the struggles of death; we didn't inflict death upon them. I should have noticed, but I failed to. I'd released her to traverse the spiritual realm as I braced myself for the last death I would withstand as a soul chaser. With Raven's soul being free of her body, I'd taken control with ease. I wouldn't have to learn the details of her life as I had with the others; her death would proceed rather quickly for me, and the process would be complete.

I wouldn't have to endure the horrendous pain of dying anymore; I'd paid my dues. I'd died for a countless number of children, and it was now time to pass the responsibility to someone else. I was a guide now, and as a guide I would be faced with a host of new challenges of my own in this transition. I would be the one in authority probing the realm, searching for the next child who would be facing an impending death. I would be the one who was risking my deliverance to the heavens and being held accountable if mistakes were made. I would be the one who oversaw Raven's journey to ensure she followed the appropriate laws, and I was now the one to impose the appropriate punishment because she had failed to comply. I would enforce the laws as Marcus had enforced them on me. She could be warned just once; her destiny would become her decision, not mine.

Becoming a guide had subjected me to hardships I'd never had to face before, but it had also rewarded me with advancement; my success as a soul chaser was a testament to my skill and ability to lead Raven on a successful journey of her own. In the beginning I watched her carefully, and she'd been triumphant; she'd followed the appropriate laws required. She'd refrained from emotional involvement, and she'd not retained memories of the departing children as instructed. However, in time she'd started demonstrating a difficulty in following *any* law. I'd never felt compassion for the children as a soul chaser. I was dying in their place, permitting their spirits to move on to the heavens, and I'd certainly never desired to relive their deaths. This was a destiny with a grand purpose, and Raven had to learn to accept that. She would have to discover selflessness.

After much deliberation I'd come to the alarming conclusion that without a warning she would be jeopardizing not only her salvation but mine as well. I had expected that I'd be able to find some sort of understanding for the negligence she demonstrated, but I'd found none. She would have to be reminded of the consequence of violating the rules, and unfortunately I'd decided that the only way to correct her behavior was to impose her first and only warning and allow her to choose the destiny that awaited her. Raven would experience her own death as the next departing child I chose.

11

FULL CIRCLE

Lucas had warned me that if I failed to follow the rules, I would be facing my own death, but I could have never imagined that I could be the one issuing the punishment...

My life as Elijah was over; the injuries his little body sustained during the horrible accident all but ensured I would flash again. He'd survived for five years battling leukemia only to have his life stripped away in the end. I'd died yet again for another innocent child, and I was finding it harder to tolerate. The violence of the most recent deaths I'd faced was taking its toll on my spirit. I was tired, tired of dying, tired of feeling sadness, and most importantly, I was tired of not understanding why I'd been chosen, or cursed. I was aware that my destiny had a purpose I didn't fully understand, but if I could have chosen this life, would I? Soon I would be faced with that very decision, and my choice would change the course of my existence *forever*.

The moment I felt the presence of people calmly milling about, I opened my eyes. I was hopeful that I'd find myself in a tranquil situation this time, or at least one that was moderately calmer than the last few days. The two deaths I last experienced had been the most emotionally impacting I'd encountered thus far. Those families had lost such young children, practically babies. How could anyone not feel compassion for those children? Their departures were heart wrenching, no matter what my destiny was. How could I possibly bear anything worse than that?

I never knew what to expect when I first opened my eyes as a new child, but what I saw this time was beyond an absolute shock. My spirit was not in a body as I had expected; I merely hovered in a room behind a pale-blue-and-white striped curtain that separated me from the child my spirit was supposed to embody. I was in a hospital room—I was certain of that; I recognized the atmosphere. Was I too late? Had I missed the opportunity to spare a child their death? I must be; why else would I emerge in the vicinity of a departing child and not inhabit their body? Could this be my punishment, knowing I was too late to offer assistance?

The compassion I'd felt for these children was nothing compared to the unbearable disappointment I now felt. I'd failed to prevent a child from experiencing the pain of death. The physical suffering this child must have endured suddenly overwhelmed me; I somehow had to find a way to offer comfort. Surely the spirit would be close by; it would be lingering in search of closure. Desperation consumed me as I willed my spirit forward, and my destiny exploded before me as the scene came into view. I was not here to spare a predetermined child his or her death; I was here to face my own. Lucas's warning was coming to pass. I'd violated too many laws, and now I would be forced to experience an emotional battle of my own as I faced the ending of my life.

As I forced my spirit to edge closer to the bed that now housed my uninhabited body, I couldn't avert my eyes from seeing all that unfolded before me. So much was happening to my lifeless body. There were tubes and wires sticking out of every orifice visible. I had a heart monitor, an IV in both of my arms, an oxygen probe on my finger and toe, electrodes stuck to both of my temples, and most important, a high-pressure medical ventilator that appeared to be forcing air into my lungs.

The doctors taking care of me had spared no expense in the attempt to keep my body alive. Unfortunately their efforts appeared to be in vain. My spirit was clearly detached from the body that lay there now; I would not be coming back. Disappointingly I had no one to come back to, as it were; I'd been abandoned at birth and spent the majority of my life in foster homes as a ward of the state. Would anyone even miss me? Paige and Thomas were the first and only parents I'd ever felt love from, and that was a façade. They weren't my parents; the love I felt from them was not intended for me but for the children my destiny took from them. No one loved me enough to take care of me while I was living, and it seemed no one loved me enough to care for me now as my body lay alone in the hospital room. Thomas and Paige loved their children, and unfortunately for me I was not their child. I'd repaid the affections I'd felt from them by fulfilling my destiny and taking their children away from them. Maybe my body should die and take my soul with it. That would be the justifiable way to pay for the betrayal I felt I'd inflicted upon those families and an honorable way to fulfill my punishment from Lucas.

When people are facing a timely death at an older age, they almost always experience visions of the life they once lived; they remember their loved ones, the many blessings they'd received, and all they'd accomplished during the course of their lives. They relived the meaningful moments of their lives in sort of a fast-forward state before death found them. Most would never realize their lives had ended until they rejoined the heavens. I, on the other hand, would know the exact moment my body died; I would relive the shivers of pain as I experienced the final moments of my life before death took my body.

The alarm blaring from the ventilator that pumped air into my lungs caught my attention immediately and brought me back to the fate that awaited me. I watched in horror as a team of medical professionals calmly walked into the room to aid my failing body. I watched them reset the alarm before checking my vitals without a hint of urgency I felt the situation warranted. As I stared at my lifeless body, I began to wonder how I'd gotten into the condition I was in. I distinctly remembered dying for Lucas, but I didn't recall an incident or accident that would have caused my spirit to detach. I must have died; my spirit was released to be a soul chaser. What happened to me, and how did my body end up alone in this hospital room?

As I allowed my spirit to inch closer, I could hear the doctor's instructions to his staff. I was instantly stunned and taken aback as I listened to him speak the words that would alter the course of my existence. "We're bringing her out of the coma this afternoon; it's been five weeks, and the swelling has gone down significantly. Her brain activity has become more frequent in the last few days, and the surge an hour ago is a good sign that the damage done during the drowning accident was minimal."

A coma! I wasn't dead? How was this even possible? I'd been in a drowning accident. Five weeks ago. *No! Wait! Wait, this doesn't make sense; I drowned for Lucas!* That was the beginning of my journey; his was the first soul I died for. Chaotic thoughts started to spin uncontrollably around my memories as my life began to unravel before me. Without warning, the horrifying reality crept in; I was dying. The first death of my journey was not Lucas's at all but the death he'd spared me from. His death was my birth into the life of soul chasing, and as horrific as it was, it was still the one significant moment I held on to, the one brief moment our souls crossed paths. I'd based the entire existence of this life on that moment, and I'd never thought to question it. What I believed to be a burden, or curse, was in fact a magnificent blessing. I'd been disregarded at birth but chosen in death. Lucas had spared me the pain of dying. He'd done for me what I'd done for so many others; he'd intercepted my death and allowed my spirit to move on. He'd spared me an eternity of isolation. If my body had died with my spirit intact, I would have been a displaced soul wandering the earth, searching for closure I would never find. He gave my life worth and me an opportunity to serve a purpose I'd failed to obtain while I was among the living—and I'd forsaken him. I'd violated our laws, and now I would be the one having to die to fulfill the destiny Lucas had chosen for me. I would not forsake him in death.

12

MY CHOICE

A sense of excitement settled over the room as Dr. Plaster and his staff prepared for my resurrection, as he called it. This would be his first attempt at bringing back the dead; my brain had shown no activity for weeks, but he wouldn't give up on me. He'd told this story so many times during the last few hours, I could nearly recite it myself:

"Female patient, approximately sixteen years old, came in unconscious from a traumatic drowning accident, weak pulse and unresponsive. CPR was done at the scene and en route, and intubation was done by the flight crew. The ER attending said her prognosis was bleak; the deprivation of oxygen was too great, and she'd be lucky to make it through the night. She was placed into a medical coma to allow the swelling to subside, and her fate was placed into my hands. Against my colleagues' recommendations and the odds stacked against her, here we are now." Dr. Plaster thought of himself as heroic. He was sure he had singlehandedly saved my life and that people would think of him as such.

Dr. Jonathon Plaster was a middle-aged man. His hair was jet black with a hint of gray, and his eyes were so dark brown they almost appeared black. He was extremely tall and athletic, a moderately attractive man with a northern accent I couldn't quite place. Dr. Plaster seemed to be highly intelligent, but his personality came off as condescending. Although his staff respected him, most of them thought of him as rude and heartless. I'd heard their versions of my miracle as well. I, however, had no opinion of him. He'd attempted to save my life, and I appreciated his efforts, but my choice was made. I could not allow my spirit to rejoin my body; I would fight for the destiny Lucas chose for me.

Six weeks ago I'd never thought about dying. I was a typical teenager living an undesirable life, but death and the afterlife were not on my mind. Lately, however, death was all I thought about. I'd died for Summer and Elijah, feeling sadness for the loss of lives. I felt I was cheating them of their liveliness, I never thought about the blessing I was offering them. If those children had perished with their spirits embodied within them, their outcome would have been far different from what it was now. Their liveliness would have been damnation. I spared those children an eternity of bewilderment as Lucas had me; I finally understood that. My journey had meaning; my existence finally had meaning. Seeing my body alone and lifeless had opened my eyes to the opportunity I'd been given. Lucas had chosen me to endure the deaths of these children, not as a punishment but as a privilege. I would never feel loneliness again, and the empathy I felt for these children would be replaced by pride and purpose as a complete acceptance flooded over me: my presence would always matter to someone.

As Dr. Plaster made his final preparations for my resurgence, a wave of uncertainty flooded over me. My human existence was over, but my spiritual journey had just begun. When my body failed, my spirit should be freed to resume the life I was chosen for. I was a soul chaser, and my destiny was now clear. However, if Lucas decided the violations were too vast, my fate might be condemnation. Would I be subjected to purgatory for eternity, or would I perhaps simply cease to exist? Had others failed him, or was I the first failure? Could a replacement be chosen for me, or had a replacement already been chosen? More questions than answers unfolded before me, but the uncertainty could not alter my decision. The death of my body could mean the end of my life, or it could become the awakening of my salvation. I would gladly wager the risk for redemption and the opportunity to spare another child.

As I hovered next to the body I'd known for sixteen years, I once again thought about Summer and Elijah and the emotions I'd experienced during the final moments of their lives. I'd never before been fearful of death; I was dying for someone else. This time, however, I would be observing the end of my own life, and I was becoming increasingly apprehensive. Could I face death without compassion? Would I be able to? I died for those children not fully understanding my journey or the consequences of the violations. Could I graciously die, selfless, as the laws required?

I watched intensely as the barbiturates used to administer my coma were reduced. The procedure could take as little as a few hours or as long as a few days according to the doctor, but he was hopeful the former applied in my case. Dr. Plaster could hardly contain his exhilaration as the rapid movement behind my eyelids began, and when the involuntary twitch of my right finger started, he spoke my name. "Raven?" I instantly felt my soul being drawn toward the body, my spirit detached from weeks ago. *Lucas drowned for me. I'm supposed to be dead; I was dead. Why was my body spared?* I would have to fight this. Death had always found me too easily, but as I listened cautiously as my heart rate slowly started to climb to a normal rhythm, the panic took hold.

Death is a place of uncertainty until you've faced it, but life can be just as unpredictable. I could choose to die and cease to exist, or I could choose to live and risk never discovering the purpose of my life. *I choose the destiny I was born to behold! Lucas, I choose selflessness.*

No sooner than I registered the thought, my body started to violently shake uncontrollably and my heartbeat leaped to an erratic pace. I was going to die as I had lived my life—alone. As Dr. Plaster desperately called out to me again, I felt my spirit being drawn closer to the body I'd chosen to abandon; however, this time I wasn't alone.

Every time he spoke my name, the spirit of a child I'd spared filled me with strength. Strength of admiration, appreciation, and acceptance for the life I'd lived. I lived for sixteen years never understanding the significance of my existence, and only now, as I faced my death, was I finally able to embrace the purpose of my being. I was born to be a sacrificial lamb. I was chosen to protect children from the pain of dying, and I would do so, forevermore—selfless. These children had not died in vain as I'd feared; they died to fulfill my destiny.

Watching my body die that afternoon, I finally accepted my death and my destiny. I realized that I was not only *chosen* to be a soul chaser, I was *born* to be one. I'm sixteen-year-old Raven Bishop, and I choose to live—as a soul chaser. Flash!

EPILOGUE

Daisies, lilies, and orchids are such distinctive fragrances, but I can smell each one of them separately. I can hear a woman's voice, so caring and warm but strained. I can hear music playing, a familiar tune I've heard before. *Think, Raven, what's that song and why does it remind you of something? Open your eyes and look around. Where am I? Why can't I think? What's happening to me? I'm so cold and closed in; am I trapped?* I can't move, and it's dark. "Help me," I begin, but no noise escapes my mouth. Panic develops in my core, but the anxiety doesn't yet consume me.

I hear a new voice, a man's voice. He's speaking of me. *Focus! What is it he's saying?*

"Raven Bishop was such a beautiful young woman, a devoted friend with so much to offer. What a travesty for the world to lose her at a mere sixteen years old. Please bow your heads and join me in a pray for our dear, sweet Raven."

The words ran around in my head as I tried to make sense of them. Did he say "was a beautiful young woman...lost me at sixteen?" *Oh God, he's giving my eulogy, but I'm not dead. Help me! Help me!* This time the panic takes hold, and all the senses I had moments ago evade me now. I can't smell, I can't hear, I feel myself slipping. *I'm not dead; someone please help me. Lucas, I'm not dead.* As the sheer panic takes over, my mind starts spinning. I feel my consciousness fading away. I try to get a grip on something, anything, a thought or a memory, something to concentrate on. I can't give in or I could be lost forever. I take a deep breath, exhale, and drift to the unknown. Flash!

Opening my eyes this time as a new person, I realized my punishment for disobedience was paid. Lucas had given me another chance and I vow to *never* squander the opportunity again. I will live on spiritually as a soul chaser, sparing innocent children from the pain of death until I, too become a guide and allow Lucas to go on to the afterlife. I will continue to have compassion but now, that I find honor in the sacrifices, the compassion I feel, will be felt for the heavens for the opportunity we are all given.

ACKNOWLEDGMENTS

To my supportive and devoted mother, Rhonda, thank you for pushing me to always pursue my dreams and for listening to my madness during our countless late-night phone calls. I love you more than *words* will ever be able to say. I love you, Mom.

To my incredibly amazing husband, Tim, thank you for believing in me and supporting me during my obsessive journey to chase the passion I've always held dear. You're my rock, and I wouldn't be me without you. I love you, babe.

To Kelsey, Tristin, Tanner, and Hanna, you kids are my world, and I'm truly blessed to be your momma. I love you.